2/21

A WHALE OF A MISTAKE

Ioana Hobai

PAGE
STREET
KiDS

"Oh!"

You made a mistake.

You worry.

The more you worry,

the more it grows, until

it weighs you down.

And then . . .

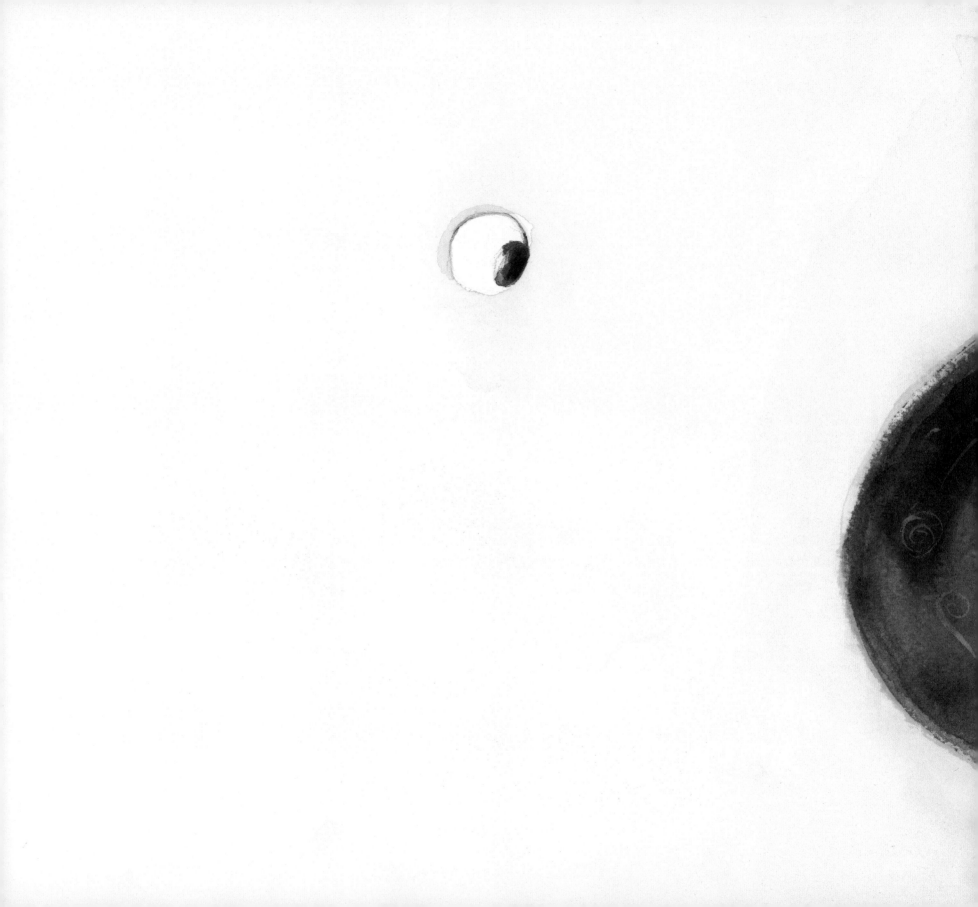

People shake their heads.
"What a big mistake!" they say.

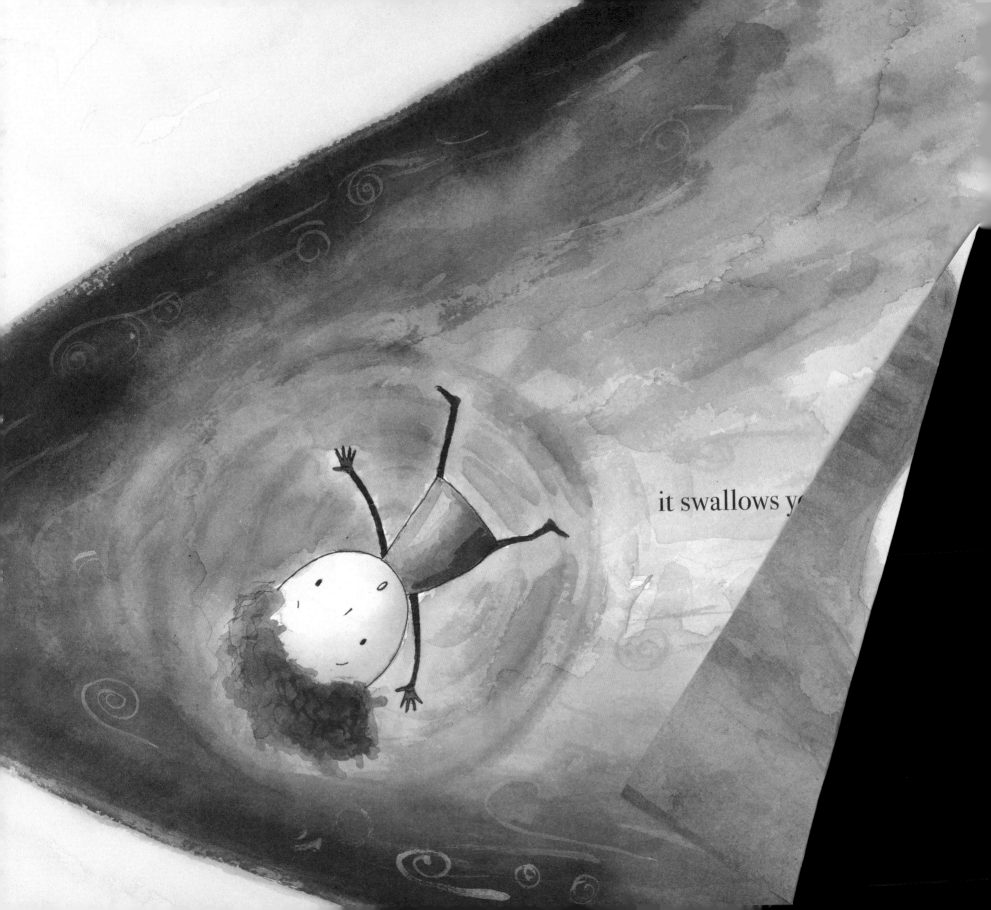

it swallows y

You shout, "Leave me alone!"
but the mistake doesn't
listen to you.

No matter what you do,
you still feel it with you.

"I can never escape it. This is my life now."

You don't know where your mistake is taking you,
but you'll have to go along for the ride.

It's not an easy ride.
You're terrified and unsure.

But when you finally gather the
courage to open your eyes . . .

you are surrounded by stars.

And they are perfect.

Or are they?

You notice that some are falling.

Are they mistakes too?

There's a whole universe
of mistakes out there.

Somehow, your mistake doesn't seem so big anymore.

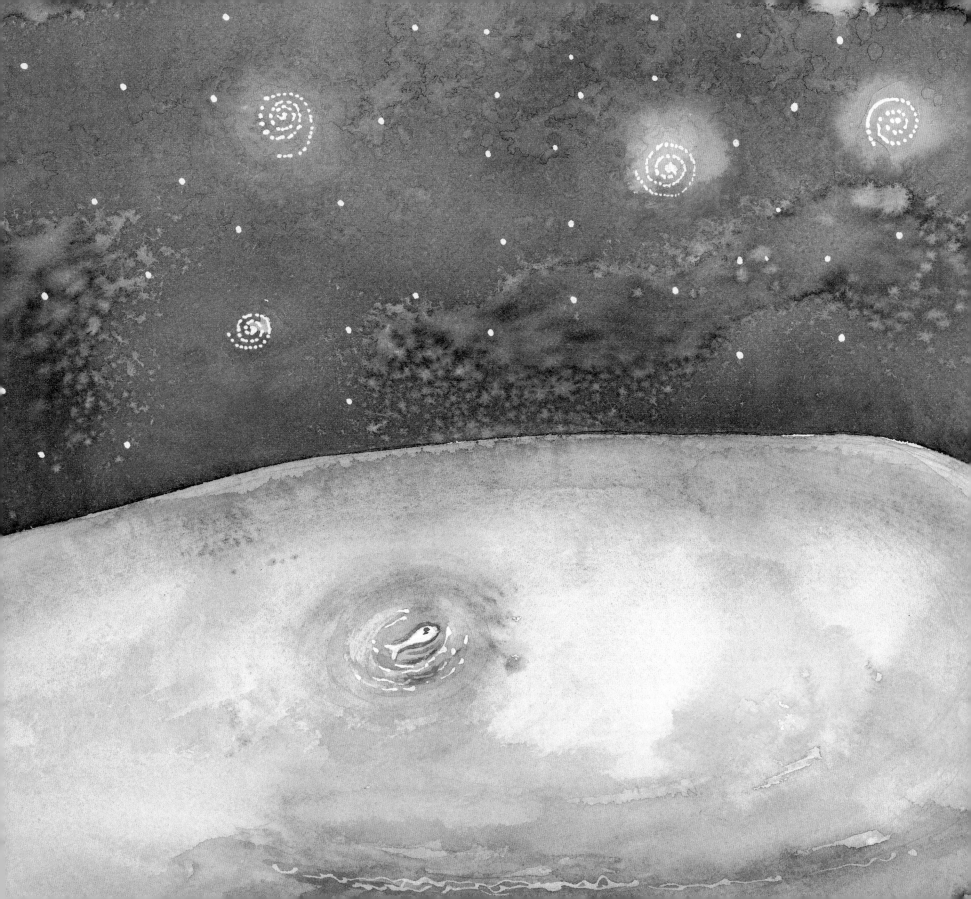

You start moving again. But now you're in control,
even if you're not yet sure of your destination.

When you're feeling brave enough to move on,
your mistake doesn't stop you anymore.

You wave goodbye and your mistake waves back,

fading wave after wave after wave . . .

For my sister Cristina, with all my love.

Page Street Publishing uses only materials from suppliers who are committed to responsible and sustainable forest management. Page Street Publishing protects our planet by donating to nonprofits like The Trustees, which focuses on local land conservation

t trustees